Ash Boy

LUCY COATS

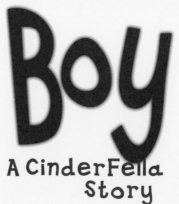

A CinderFella
Story

With illustrations by
Mark Beech

Barrington 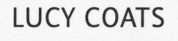 Stoke

First published in 2017 in Great Britain by
Barrington Stoke Ltd
18 Walker Street, Edinburgh, EH3 7LP

www.barringtonstoke.co.uk

Text © 2017 Lucy Coats
Illustrations © 2017 Mark Beech

A CIP catalogue record for this book is available
from the British Library upon request

ISBN: 978-1-78112-718-6

Printed in China by Leo

*To all the fab librarians out there,
but especially Barbara Band, Joy Court,
Annie Everall and Dawn Finch*

Contents

Chapter 1
Pots and Pans

My name is Cinder Ashok.

I was 13 when Mum died in a freak accident. Back then I was sure it was the most dreadful thing that would ever happen to me. I didn't think life could get any worse. I was wrong.

Only a few weeks after Mum's funeral, just as I'd learned to make scrambled eggs that weren't totally burned, Dad said he had something to tell me. He was marrying Mrs Karim from 27 Ember Street, and I'd have two nice new step-brothers. We'd be a proper family again, he said.

"How could you, Dad?" I yelled. "What would Mum say? And those horrible Karim boys are the ones who threw me into the pond when I was little, remember? I would have drowned if Buttons hadn't fished me out."

Buttons is my best friend – she's a mad comic book addict just like me. We hang out together most days in the library – my favourite place in the whole world. Buttons is really cool, with a shock of bright blue hair.

But she's a bit annoying too, like the way she's always so mysterious about where she lives.

I have to admit, I'm pretty UNcool. I've got long skinny legs, no muscles to show off, and square black glasses with thick lenses.

When Dad saw I was upset, he tried his best comforting voice on me.

"I'm sure you'll get on with Rock and Boulder now you're older, Cinder," he said. "And Mrs Karim is lovely. So kind. I know you miss Mum, but this way you'll have a new family to love. It'll all be fine."

*

But it wasn't fine. The minute the wedding was over, the trouble began. My new stepmother threw out all Mum's pretty things and started spending money like it was going out of fashion. And that means Dad has to go away on business more and more to pay for it all, and I never see him.

As for me, I never have time for the library or books or Buttons now. I'm always stuck in the house. I wash filthy dishes, sweep out ashy fireplaces and polish heavy suits of armour.

The rest of the time I'm in the stables, where I muck out smelly piles of horse poo, and brush mud off Rock and Boulder's battle horses. Those two are turning out to be worse bullies than ever, of course.

Did I mention that my big ugly step-brothers have big ugly ambitions?

They want to serve Prince Charmless in his rough and rowdy Palace Guard – but everyone knows only the best fighters get in. When they aren't bashing each other with their swords, or galloping around with spears, they start on me.

The first day's fun started with them grabbing me from behind.

"Come on, Ash Boy," they yelled. "Time for target practice!"

I struggled, but it was no good. Rock crammed a metal pot on my head, and Boulder pushed the handle of a saucepan lid over one

of my hands. Then they took me outside, tied
me to a post and made me hold out this tiny
wooden hoop. After that, they took turns
running at me with their lances. It was SCARY.

"You'll break my g-glasses," I wailed, as
the first lance missed the hoop and hit my
saucepan-lid shield.

But those bullies just laughed, and kicked their horses on even faster.

By the time they finished, I was covered in bruises. As I crept into my attic bed that night, I had a bad feeling that worse was to come.

Chapter 2
A Royal Invitation

How right I was.

The very next day, a Royal footman in a white wig delivered a letter to us. My stepmother dismissed the man with a snooty wave of her hand.

Then she screeched with joy as she opened the letter.

"Look! Look, boys!"

Rock and Boulder pushed past me and clanked in. I was on my knees at the time, scrubbing the hall floor.

"What, Ma?" they asked, but she was already waving a square of black card under their noses. I got up and stood on tiptoe to see past the beefy brothers.

**The King, Queen
and Prince Charmless invite**

Mr and Mrs Ashok and family to a
Grand Quintain Contest

—⟁ for ⟁—

The Princess Betony's
14th Birthday

The winner of the Grand Quintain
Contest will be granted a favour of their
choice by the Princess.

The posh gold letters sparkled in the sunshine that poured in the open front door.

"Wow! This is our chance to impress Prince Charmless," Rock yelled, and he punched Boulder in the arm.

"Yay, Bro!" Rock shouted, and they headed back out to the stable yard. They kicked over my bucket of dirty water on purpose as they passed.

"Clean that up, you clumsy boy," my stepmother said. But her greedy eyes were full of dreams about hob-nobbing with royalty.

*

From that moment on, my life wasn't worth living.

Dad was away again on a long trip, so the three horrors kept me up till all hours, polishing and cleaning. The whole house was full of dress-makers, hat-makers, shoe-makers and armour-makers. Rock and Boulder bought not one, but two new battle horses each.

All I heard from morning to night was –

"Do this!"

"Do that!"

"Where's my sword?"

"Why is there dirt on my saddle?"

"GET HERE, ASH BOY!"

I was worn out – but not too worn out to dream a few dreams of my own.

What if I entered the Grand Quintain Contest?

What if I won?

What favour would I ask for from Princess Betony?

I knew exactly what I'd ask for, of course.

I'd always dreamed I could be a librarian one day. I loved to be surrounded by books, or chatting to Buttons about them. I loved the smell of books, and when I read the stories inside, it was like walking into a new world all of my own. I missed the library and Buttons so much it hurt.

Then I looked down at my skinny arms and legs and sighed. How could *I* win a contest against Rock and Boulder, let alone all Prince Charmless's men-at-arms? I didn't have a horse, or armour, or any fighting skills at all. But as I ran around trying to keep up with my never-ending list of chores, the idea took hold of me and wouldn't let go.

I was going to enter the Grand Quintain Contest.

Chapter 3
More Bad News

Rock and Boulder stepped up their quintain training from frantic to manic, and I began to watch and listen. It all seemed so silly. The important thing was to put a big stick into a tiny ring about a hundred times. How on earth did that prove you were a great warrior?

But I wanted to escape from my current life more than anything – and if I could win that favour from Princess Betony, perhaps I could do it. Maybe Dad would buy me some proper kit when he got back. But until he returned, I'd have to work with what I'd got.

What I had was Silver, my old rocking horse. He lived in the attic along with some rats, a lot of mice, and too many spiders to count. Silver had been there ever since my wicked stepmother got rid of all my old toys.

"You don't need this rubbish any more," she told me. "You're not a baby."

And after that, I was sent off to the attic too. Rock needed my old bedroom to keep his spare armour in. Rock has a LOT of spare armour.

And so I armed myself with a feather
duster, a mop handle, some tape and wire and
the biggest darning needle I could find.

I dusted all the cobwebs off Silver,
apologising to the spiders as I went. Then I
stuck the darning needle sideways into a beam
in the attic roof, and taped the wire to the mop
handle.

"Come on, boy," I said, and I climbed onto Silver. "Here goes."

It took me four nights even to touch the needle with the wire, and another two to get the wire into the needle. But by the week before the Grand Quintain Contest I could do it every single time, with my eyes closed.

The rest of my plan wasn't going so well. Where was Dad? Why wasn't he home from sea? Time was running out.

I looked out of the window at each carriage that passed. But Dad wasn't in any of them. How was my dream ever going to come true now? I couldn't take an old rocking horse to the contest – I'd be a laughing stock.

And then, the evening before the Grand Quintain Contest, a messenger galloped up to our front door and pounded on it with his fist.

"Letter for the Widow Ashok," he panted, and he crammed it into my hand.

I couldn't make sense of his words at first. My body trembled with fear. What had he called her – the *Widow* Ashok?

Then my stepmother snatched the damp letter off me and ripped it open. "Your stupid, stupid father," she snarled, and she threw her cup and saucer at the wall. "He's only gone and got himself drowned."

My heart stopped in my chest. When it started up again, it felt as if someone had ripped it in two. I bent down like a very old person. I picked up the letter and read it.

I am sorry to report that the Albatross *went down in a storm. She went down with all hands. The owner, Mr Asif Ashok, was on board. We have found no survivors.*

I knew now that THIS was the most dreadful thing that had ever happened to me. I had no Mum or Dad, nobody in the world. I was an orphan, all alone.

Chapter 4
999 Fairy

I cried. I admit it. I cried till my face was stiff with salt and my throat felt as if I'd never breathe again. Dad might not have been around much, but he was still my dad, and now he and Mum were gone for ever. The only thing I had left of them was a little silver locket. Just before dawn I slipped into a doze, clutching it to my heart.

It seemed like seconds later when I was woken by a slap in the face from a cold, wet sponge.

"Up! Up, you lazy toad," my step-brothers shouted at me. "There's work to do. We must be at the Palace on time."

I blanked out their chatter as I stumbled about my chores. I knew none of the three horrors cared about Dad, but they could at least have pretended. There wasn't so much as a black armband in sight when they left for their day of triumph. My stepmother was

a-flutter in pink silk and feathers and Rock and Boulder shone in their armour over the finest sky-blue velvet.

They locked me in, of course.

"Polish all the silver and clean up that broken china I chucked at the wall," my stepmother shouted as she clambered into her carriage.

"Loser! Loser! *Double loser!*" Rock and Boulder yelled as they galloped off.

If I could have magicked a monster to swallow them up, I would have. 'It's a shame,' I thought, 'that magic doesn't exist.'

*

As soon as they were out of sight my legs went wobbly and I sat down in a heap in the middle of the kitchen. I pulled my locket over my head and stared at the two tiny portraits inside.

There was Dad, with that lock of black hair that always fell over his left eye. Mum looked at him, all smiles and dimples.

That's when I decided to run away. There was nothing here for me now. I closed the locket and blinked hard. A tear slid down my cheek and fell onto the silver locket. It opened with a tiny click. That was odd – Mum and Dad's pictures were gone. There were some

words there instead, in curly, old-fashioned
writing. I read –

In desperate trouble?
Set saucepan to bubble.
Throw in something hairy.
Say "999 FAIRY".

I cleaned my glasses and looked again. The
words were still there. Well, I *was* in desperate
trouble, wasn't I? I was too old to believe in
magic or fairies or spells, but I'd give anything
a go.

I ran to the kitchen, filled a pot with water,
blew up the fire to hot, and set the pot to boil.
Then I got a sharp knife and cut off a curl of my
black hair. As soon as the water was bubbling,
I hurled the hair in.

"999 fairy," I whispered. I felt a bit silly, and
a bit hopeful.

Nothing.

I said it again, a bit louder. "999 FAIRY."

Still nothing.

That last tiny bit of hope I'd had ran out like sand through my fingers.

Chapter 5
Tinker

WHY wouldn't the spell work? It was SO unfair.
I knew it was no use, but I gave it one last go.

"999 FAIRY!" I bellowed at the pot, so loud
that the plates in the sink rattled.

The flames went out with a hiss as the pot
spun and jumped in the air. My jaw hit the
floor as a stream of purple smoke poured out
and shaped itself into a silver door in the air.
The door opened with a loud creak and out
stepped the strangest person I'd ever seen.

He was tall and thin, with flowing hair
like embers, and he was wearing robes which

seemed to be made of orange mist. His golden
cat-eyes were lined with black, and in his
pointy ears he wore huge gold hoops studded
with rubies. He jumped down to the floor as
quiet as a cat.

"Hello, Cinder Ashok," he said. "I'm Tinker,
your Fairy Godfather. How can I help?"

It took several moments for me to get any words out, and when I did they were garbled.

"W-what? W-who? H-how?" I babbled.

Tinker narrowed his eyes at me.

"Hush," he said, and he put his long fingers on my head. With a *whoosh*, all the memories of everything that had happened since Mum and Dad died lit up in my brain.

"By my ears," my Fairy Godfather said. "You *have* had a bad time. But don't worry. I'm here to fix all that. You SHALL go to the Grand Quintain Contest, Cinder Ashok, but we need to hurry." He pulled a stick like a twisty rainbow out of his robes. "Let's start with your armour and lance, shall we?"

Faster than I could say *comic book*, Tinker had draped me in a dishcloth, put a wooden spoon in my hand and waved his twisty stick at me. One rainbow flash later, I was in golden

armour from head to foot. It was light as air,
and it fitted my body like a glove.

"Wow!" I said. I twirled my new lance and
almost knocked the casserole dishes over. This
was SO cool. I felt like one of my comic book
superheroes.

"You'll need something to ride as well,"
Tinker said, and he waved his twisty stick
again.

I heard a clatter of hooves coming down the stairs.

"What –?" I didn't have time to finish. A huge grey battle horse trotted into the kitchen.

"Is that …?" It was odd, but the horse looked like my old Silver.

"There's no time, no time," Tinker said. He took the horse by the reins and led him out of the door. "Up you get," he said to me. "Steady now."

I clambered up and set my feet in the golden stirrups.

"You can't fall off, and your lance won't break," Tinker said. "But you MUST be back here by sunset, or everything will turn back to what it was before. Good luck, Cinder."

With that, Tinker slapped Silver on the rump and off we went.

Silver and I galloped to the Palace like a tornado was behind us. We skidded to a halt in front of a big table with a sign on it. The sign said –

**ENTER THE GRAND QUINTAIN
CONTEST HERE**

"Name?" a large bearded man demanded.

I panicked. I couldn't say Cinder Ashok. What should I call myself?

"G-Golden Knight," I stammered out.

The man sniggered as he scribbled my new name on a form.

"Very well, little Golden Knight," he said. "Last in is first to compete. You're just in time."

Chapter 6
The Grand Quintain Contest

I couldn't see much after I'd put the visor on
my helmet down. I peered out of the eye slits
and could just make out the blur of the Royal
Box, high above the crowd. The box was draped
in red velvet, and the Royal Family looked
like tiny blobs inside. I bowed to them, and
clutched my lance under one arm, as I'd seen
Rock and Boulder do so many times.

The heralds' trumpets sounded, and I began
to shake. What was I doing here? I could
hardly even see the quintain ring.

"First contestants!" a voice bellowed.
"Please welcome Sir Roger de Coverley and

the … er … rather small Golden Knight. Golden Knight goes first."

I listened as titters and jeers ran along the crowd like a wave. Somehow it made me brave. I'd show them.

"Giddy up, Silver," I said. "Let's go!"

Silver whinnied as he sped into a flat-out gallop.

I didn't know if it was all the practice I'd done with the mop handle and darning needle or a touch of Tinker's magic, but my lance went straight into the ring.

Sir Roger went next and missed.

"Golden Knight wins the first match," the marshal cried. He sounded surprised. The crowd gave a muted cheer.

As the rounds went on, I kept on winning. When I beat Rock in the tenth round the crowd really got on my side.

"GOL-DEN KNIGHT! GOL-DEN KNIGHT!" they chanted. What a sound! It felt really good.

The rings got smaller and smaller as the contest went on. The final ring was the tiniest of all, and my opponent in that round was Boulder. He barged his horse up against Silver and stuck an elbow into me.

"No chance, skinnyshanks," he jeered.

The crowd booed as he galloped away and ... he missed the ring.

I squeezed my eyes shut for a second as Silver and I set off. It was now or never. Do or die!

The crowd's roar told me I'd won. They pulled me down off Silver and carried me on their shoulders up to the Royal Box to collect my favour from the princess. As I stumbled in front of her, I had two huge shocks.

1. Princess Betony was my best friend, Buttons. She didn't have her blue hair, but I recognised her anyway.

2. The sky wasn't blue any more – the sun was about to set. I had to get home before the magic ended.

What should I do? I bent forward and whispered the name of our favourite comic book superhero into Princess Betony's ear. As her mouth fell open in surprise, I tugged off one of my golden gloves, flung it into her lap and vaulted down from the box onto Silver's back.

"Home, boy!" I yelled. I prayed that Silver wouldn't turn back into a rocking horse in front of everyone. How embarrassing would THAT be?

*

We just made it. I dragged my noble wooden steed into the shed and hid him. Then I ran for the kitchen with my dishcloth and wooden spoon. I had just locked the door when I heard the swish of carriage wheels and the voice of an angry stepmother.

"How could you lose to that stupid Golden Knight, you idiots?" she yelled at Rock and Boulder as she slammed the carriage door and swept into the house.

"As for you," she said, and she glared at me from under her big pink hat. "You can be on bread and water for a week. That'll teach you to obey orders." She kicked at the broken china which still littered the floor.

All the joy I'd felt at winning drained out of me in an instant. I was now in an even worse mess than before.

Chapter 7
The Royal Decree

As I swept the kitchen floor, I thought about Princess Betony.

I still couldn't quite believe that she was my friend Buttons. Was Buttons' blue hair a wig? If she was the princess, it was no wonder she'd always been so mysterious about where she lived. But how was I going to tell her that I was the Golden Knight when I was stuck in the house with a stack of horrible chores to do? I just had to hope my golden glove had survived the sunset, and that Betony – I mean Buttons – would understand the clue I'd given her.

The very next day I heard news of a Royal
Decree.

"OYEZ! OYEZ!" a herald shouted in the
square outside our house. "Be it known that
the Princess Betony will visit every home in
the land in search of the Knight of the Golden
Glove. He who fits the glove and answers the
Royal question will win the Princess's favour."

I couldn't wait for her to knock on our door. It made all the shouting, the kickings and the meals of bread and water almost bearable.

But when the Royal party turned up a week later, my stepmother pushed me up the narrow stairs to the attic.

"Stay there," she hissed. "Don't make a sound, or I'll twist your nose off and make you more sorry than you've ever been in your life."

As the key turned in the lock, I slumped to the floor in despair. Now Buttons would never find me.

But after a few minutes a clear voice floated up from the ground floor.

"Where is Cinder Ashok?"

It WAS Buttons.

"I know he lives in this house," the voice declared. "It says so on the Royal census."

"Nobody of that name here, Your Royalness," Rock and Boulder grovelled.

"Don't lie," Buttons snapped.

"He's just a servant, Your Highness," my stepmother said. "No need to bother with him."

"Fetch him," Buttons said. "Right now."

The sound of the key turning in my attic door was like a miracle. I ran downstairs past my stepmother's freezing glare and put my finger to my lips as I saw Buttons wink at me. I knew we couldn't reveal that we were friends just yet.

Rock was trying on the golden glove. It wouldn't fit over his big, beefy hand, of course.

"Give it here, stupid," Boulder said.

Blood was dripping from Boulder's hand. Was he so desperate to win that he'd chopped off his own finger tips?

"Ugh!" Buttons said, when she saw the blood.
"No way are you the winner. Give the glove to
Cinder."

Boulder flung the glove at me and ran out of the room bellowing and snarling. I didn't know or care whether it was pain or rage.

I shook the blood off the glove and slid it on. My stepmother and Rock howled with dismay and Buttons stepped forward.

"Now for the Royal question," she said, and a little smile played at the corner of her mouth. "Who can be killed by Kryptonite?"

Chapter 8

Superman

It was an answer for a comic book fan – and I'd whispered it in Buttons' ear before I left the Royal Box. Now I knew why Buttons had always been so obsessed with Clark Kent's disguise. She'd been in disguise herself all along.

"Superman," I said, as the golden glove fizzed and disappeared into thin air.

"And Clark Kent wins the day again!" we yelled together. We jumped up and bumped fists.

That was when the madness started.

My awful stepmother flew at Buttons in such a rage that the Royal Guard had to hold her back. As for my ugly step-brothers, they got me in a head-lock and tried to strangle me. The herald set me free by knocking them out with his trumpet.

The guards took the three horrors off to the castle dungeon where they were charged with a string of crimes, from unlawful imprisonment of a family member to assault on a Royal princess.

In the meantime, I explained everything to Buttons. Well, everything except how I got my horse and armour. I didn't want her to laugh at me, and a fairy godfather was a bit embarrassing, however useful and nice he might be.

"What do you want as your favour, then?" Buttons asked. "You won the quintain contest fair and square."

I took a deep breath.

"All I want is to work in the town library," I said. "And be left in peace by my stepmother and step-brothers –"

Buttons laughed – but it was a nice laugh.

"I think we can do a bit better than that," she said. "Why don't you come and work for my mum and dad and be Librarian-in-Chief of the Royal Library?"

That sounded like every dream I'd ever had all rolled into one. I went to hug Buttons but then I stopped. I didn't think the stern Royal Herald would approve.

"Why did you always use the town library if you had a Royal one?" I asked Buttons instead.

"Because the Royal Library only has stuffy old books with tiny print," Buttons told me. "And I can't read them very well. The letters go all squizzy when I look at them. That's why I like comics best. If you're the Royal Librarian you might order some books I want to read. Come on, Cinder. I'll give you a tour and you can start as soon as you've had something to eat. You look half starved."

"I'll get right on it," I promised, as Buttons pulled me over to her smart carriage.

"Don't you think Mr Ashok should ... well ... wash first, Your Royal Highness?" the Royal Herald asked. "He's a bit, ahem, grubby."

It was true. My clothes were ragged and dirty, and my ashy hands were a disgrace.

"I don't care," Buttons said. "What's a little dirt between best friends?"

As I climbed into the carriage, I saw a flash of twisty rainbow light out of the corner of my eye. Then Buttons gasped, and her eyes went as round as pebbles.

"Y-your clothes," she said. "What's happened?"

I looked down and saw that I was now dressed in a suit fit for the King himself, and I was cleaner than a polished plate. There was no help for it. I'd have to confess.

"Let me tell you about my fairy godfather," I said.

Our books are tested
for children and young people by
children and young people.

Thanks to everyone who consulted on
a manuscript for their time and effort in
helping us to make our books better
for our readers.

If you enjoyed this zany adventure, you'll love ...

As a rule, Shona doesn't hate any living
thing, but she can't stand bats. And that's
pretty unfortunate – she has a bat project
to contend with at school, PLUS there's a bat
colony in the attic! Will Shona go ... batty?

**From the winner of the
Queen's Gold Medal for Poetry.**